MOUSE LOVES FALL

by Lauren Thompson

illustrated by Buket Erdogan

Ready-to-Read

Simon Spotlight

New York   London   Toronto   Sydney   New Delhi

SIMON SPOTLIGHT
An imprint of Simon & Schuster Children's Publishing Division
1230 Avenue of the Americas, New York, New York 10020
This Simon Spotlight edition August 2018
Text copyright © 2006, 2018 by Lauren Thompson
Illustrations copyright © 2006 by Buket Erdogan
All rights reserved, including the right of reproduction in whole or in part in
any form. SIMON SPOTLIGHT, READY-TO-READ, and colophon are registered
trademarks of Simon & Schuster, Inc. For information about special discounts for
bulk purchases, please contact Simon & Schuster Special Sales at 1-866-506-1949 or
business@simonandschuster.com.
Manufactured in the United States of America 0718 LAK
10 9 8 7 6 5 4 3 2 1
Library of Congress Cataloging-in-Publication Data
Names: Thompson, Lauren, 1962– author. | Erdogan, Buket, illustrator.
Title: Mouse loves fall / by Lauren Thompson ; illustrated by Buket Erdogan.
Description: New York : Simon Spotlight, 2018. | Series: Ready-to-Read | Series:
Mouse | Summary: "On a crisp autumn day, Mouse and Minka celebrate fall by
jumping in a pile of leaves"—Provided by publisher. | Identifiers: LCCN 2018009494
| ISBN 9781534421462 (pbk) | ISBN 9781534421479 (hc) | ISBN 9781534421486
(eBook) | Subjects: | CYAC: Autumn—Fiction. | Brothers and sisters—Fiction. |
Mice—Fiction. | BISAC: JUVENILE FICTION / Readers / Beginner. | JUVENILE
FICTION / Animals / Mice, Hamsters, Guinea Pigs, etc. | JUVENILE FICTION /
Imagination & Play. | Classification: LCC PZ7.T37163 Mf 2018 | DDC [E]—dc23 | LC
record available at https://lccn.loc.gov/2018009494

The illustrations and portions of the text were previously published in 2006
in *Mouse's First Fall*.

It is a cool fall day.

Mouse and big sister Minka come out to play!

What do they see?

"Look at all the colors!"
says Minka.

Which colors does
Mouse see?

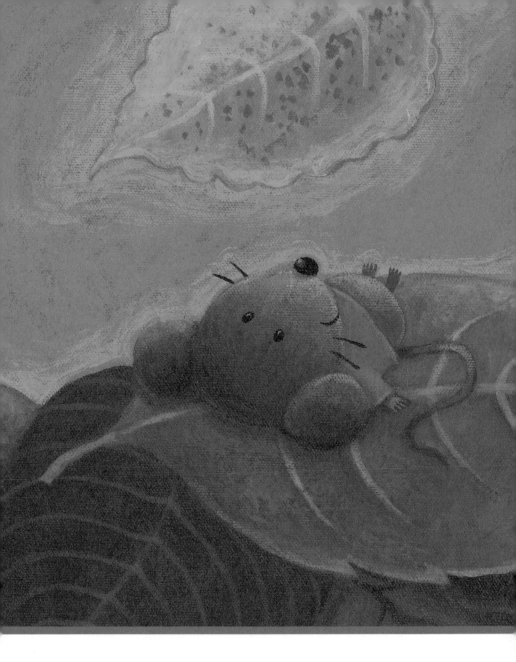

Mouse sees **red** leaves
and **yellow** leaves.

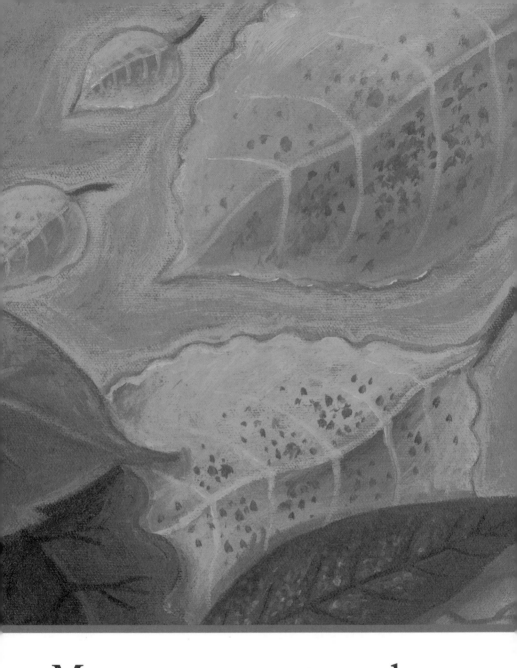

Mouse sees **orange** leaves
and **brown** leaves.
Pretty!

"Look at all the shapes!"
says Minka.

Which shapes does
Mouse see?

Mouse sees **round** leaves
and **skinny** leaves.

Mouse sees **pointy** leaves
and **smooth** leaves.
Yay!

"Run through the leaves!"
says Minka.

Mouse runs fast!

Mouse **runs** and **skips** through the leaves.

Mouse **kicks** and **swishes** through the leaves. Fun!

"Pile up the leaves!"
says Minka.

Mouse helps make
a leaf pile.

Mouse piles leaves high.

One leaf! **Two** leaves!

Three leaves!

Lots of leaves!

Yippee!

"What a big pile!"
says Minka.

"Lets jump in!"

Mouse **leaps** and **jumps** into the leaves.

Mouse **plops** and **rolls**
in the leaves.
Whee!

"I am hiding,"
calls Minka.

"Can you find me?"

Mouse **peeks** and
pokes and **peers**
between the leaves.

Where could Minka be?

Then out pops Minka!

"Here I am!"
she says.

Hooray for Minka!

Hooray for Mouse!

Hip-hip-hooray for fall!